P9-DFO-292

DETROIT PUBLIC LIBRARY

LINCOLN BRANCH LIBRARY

1221 E. SEVEN MILE

DETROIT, MI   48203

DATE DUE

jE

OCT 1 3 1994	
NOV 1 0 1994	
DEC 1 0 1993	
APR 1 3 1995	
MAY 0 7 1996	
DEC 0 5 1996	
ILL	
DEC 21 1996	
NOV 3 0 1999	

SEEDS

LINCOLN BRANCH LIBRARY
1221 E. SEVEN MILE
DETROIT, MI 48203

GEORGE SHANNON

ILLUSTRATED BY **STEVE BJÖRKMAN**

Houghton Mifflin Company

Boston 1994

LI AUG 1994

jE

Text copyright © 1994 by George Shannon
Illustrations copyright © 1994 by Steve Björkman

All rights reserved. For information about permission
to reproduce selections from this book, write to
Permissions, Houghton Mifflin Company, 215 Park Avenue
South, New York, New York 10003.

Library of Congress Cataloging-in-Publication Data

Shannon, George.
 Seeds / written by George Shannon ; illustrated by Steve
Björkman.
  p. cm.
 Summary: When Warren moves away he misses his older friend next
door and the times they shared in the garden, but the separation
inspires each of them to do something creative about it.
 ISBN 0-395-66990-1
 [1. Friendship—Fiction. 2. Gardens—Fiction. 3. Moving,
Household—Fiction.] I. Björkman, Steve, ill. II. Title.
PZ7.S5287Sg 1994 92-40738
[E]—dc20   CIP
       AC

Printed in the United States of America

BVG 10 9 8 7 6 5 4 3 2 1

To Mrs. Griswold and Warren — G.S.

For Linda, Carl, and Karen — S.B.

Every day after breakfast, but before the mail comes, Warren
looks out his window at Bill's window next door. If Bill's curtains
are open and his mother says "yes," Warren waves good-bye to
his brother and runs outside.

Warren has been Bill's helper since Bill moved in and Warren passed him nails as they built the garden fence.

"What's new?" calls Warren as he walks through the open gate.

"Look around," Bill grins. "And *you* tell me."

When Warren sees the snapdragons, he stops and turns. Bill nods, and Warren picks just one to squeeze and snap while they check the rest of the garden zoo. Larkspur rabbits. Pink turtleheads. Monkey faces in the pansies, and hens with their little chicks huddled around.

Together they look for weeds,
move baby plants, and pick wilted
flowers so more will bloom.

Then they turn on the sprinkler and run for the steps!

Some days Warren sings a new song he's learned at school or tells his story of how the snapping dragons come alive at night and chase the squirrels that dig the garden up.

Last winter, when the garden was covered with snow, they sat in Bill's back room, filled with sixty years of things his grandmother loved. When they played the riddle game, Warren's last riddle was always the same.

"What's red and blue and white?"

"Hmmmm," said Bill. "The coffee cup that looks like a bird?"

"No. *And* yellow and green."

"The basket full of postcards?"

"NO! You know! *And* black and gold and purple and pink!"

"The button jug."

"Right! You do it now."

On warm days they watch the flowers shine in the sprinkler's rain.

"Maybe," says Bill, "you can bring your little brother to see someday."

Warren looks around the yard and then at Bill.

"Not enough room."

Warren growls and makes the snapdragon snap.

"*He's* scared of dragons."

"Well," says Bill, "you decide. Time to turn off the water and send me back to my drawing board."

They look at the picture Bill is drawing for a book or magazine.
Then each chooses a cookie for a good-bye treat.

"See you later, Alligator."
"After 'while, Crocodile."

"After 'while" usually comes the next day or the day after that.

But one day it doesn't come anymore.

Warren's family moves to a big new house in another town.

Warren's new block finally has some kids his age, and the park is so close he gets to go nearly every day.

He even has a bedroom all to himself. But when he looks out the window, dirt is the only thing to see. No window to watch. No fence. No Bill. No dragons to snap or flowers to smell.

Bill doesn't have to worry about anybody stepping on the baby plants anymore. But most days the garden feels too still. No giggles. No songs. No riddle games. No stories of dragons chasing squirrels.

Bill draws Warren pictures of the garden zoo, but doesn't like any of them enough to send. They can't be smelled or picked or snapped.

Warren draws lots of pictures, too. Dragons and squirrels. Flowers and Bill with the button jug. One day Warren draws a picture of himself watering a dragon that's stuck in the dirt.

"Dumb," he says and wads it up.

Then he smooths it back out and runs to his mother with a new idea. "I have to send this and a letter to Bill so *I* can stick some dragons in the dirt!"

When a big package arrives from Bill, it has the seeds Warren asked him to send. And a lot more, too! All from Bill's garden so Warren can grow his own garden zoo. Bill's letter has a drawing of a squirrel with a watering can. "What's it say?" Warren asks, and his mother reads:

Dear Warren,

Your idea for a garden gave me an idea for a story-book. Two squirrels start a garden, then one moves away. They miss each other and one day squirrel gets <u>your</u> idea. He sends his friend seeds so both of them can share the garden again.

I hope my book is done by the time your red chrysan-themum blooms. See you later, Alligator.

Love,

Bill

Warren smiles. "After 'while, Crocodile!"

When Warren's father gets home, they mark a spot for the garden that Warren can see from his window upstairs.

And in the morning after breakfast,
Bill and Warren both go to work.

Warren in his garden

and Bill on his book.